NEARLY FEARLESS

MONKEY PIRATES

HUNT FOR THE OCTO-SHARK

A 4D BOOK

BY MICHAEL ANTHONY STEELE

ILLUSTRATED BY PAULINE REEVES

PICTURE WINDOW BOOKS
a capstone imprint

Nearly Fearless Monkey Pirates is published by Stone Arch Books,
A Capstone Imprint
1710 Roe Crest Drive
North Mankato, Minnesota 56003
www.capstonepub.com

Cataloging-in-Publication Data is available on the Library of Congress website.
ISBN: 978-1-5158-2680-4 (library binding)
ISBN: 978-1-5158-2688-0 (paperback)
ISBN: 978-1-5158-2692-7 (eBook PDF)

Summary: When his crew expresses doubts about the existence of the octo-shark,
a creature that is half octopus and half shark, Captain Banana Beard of the
Nearly Fearless Monkey Pirates and his crew set out on a hunt to find the mythical
monster—but the search nearly turns all of them into an octo-shark lunch.

Designer: Ted Williams

Design elements:
Shutterstock: Angeliki Vel, MAD SNAIL, nazlisart

Printed and bound in the USA
PA021

Download the Capstone app!

- Ask an adult to download the Capstone 4D app.

- Scan the cover and stars inside the book for additional content.

When you scan a spread, you'll find
fun extra stuff to go with this book!
You can also find these things
on the web at www.capstone4D.com
using the password: octoshark.26804

TABLE OF CONTENTS

MEET THE CREW

CAPTAIN BANANA BEARD

Captain Banana Beard is the almost-brave leader of the monkey pirates. Banana Beard often puts his search for treasure before the safety of his crew. But he's always sure to give credit where credit is due!

FIRST MATE FEZ

Wearing a red fez hat (wonder how he got his name?), Fez is in charge of the ship's charts and books. He tries to keep Captain Banana Beard's plans from getting too crazy, but that's a nearly impossible job for any monkey!

BANANA JUICE

BANANAS

CREWMAN MR. PICKLES

Mr. Pickles is the lowest on the chain of command, but he's still excited to be the best pirate he can be. With every job he does, Mr. Pickles is one step closer to being a great pirate captain, just like his hero, Captain Banana Beard.

QUARTERMASTER FOSSEY

Fossey keeps track of the ship's goods and treasure. She's in charge of all the gear and knows the supplies down to the last banana. And if the adventure calls for a certain tool that the ship doesn't have, Fossey can build it in record time.

CHAPTER 1

THE HUNT BEGINS

"Fez!" Captain Banana Beard stormed out of his cabin aboard his ship, the *Merry Monkey*. "First Mate Fez!" he yelled.

"Coming, Captain!" Fez swung through the sails. He landed in front of the bearded monkey. "Yes, sir?"

"Has the crew finished swabbing the decks?" Banana Beard asked.

Swabbing the decks was monkey-pirate talk for *scrubbing the floors.*

"I'll check, Captain," Fez replied. He looked up.

Fossey stood in the crow's nest—a basket at the top of the ship's mast. She looked through a small telescope.

"Fossey!" Fez called up. "Has the crew finished swabbing the deck?"

Fossey aimed
her telescope
downward.
"Almost finished!"
she yelled.

Fez turned
back to Captain
Banana Beard.
"Almost finished,
Captain," he said.

"Good, good," the captain
said. "Let's have a look."

The captain marched toward
the lower deck. Fez followed
close behind.

Fossey slid down a rope and landed behind them. All three monkeys marched across the main deck. They gathered around a fourth monkey, Mr. Pickles.

Mr. Pickles pushed a soapy mop across the floorboards. When he saw the captain, he stood at attention.

The captain looked around. "Well done, lad. Well done."

"Thank you, sir," Mr. Pickles said.

Just then, a half-eaten banana fell from the captain's bushy beard. It plopped onto the clean deck.

The captain looked down. "You
missed a spot, Mr. Pickles."

"That just fell from your beard,
sir," Mr. Pickles said.

"No, it didn't," the captain said. "I don't keep bananas in me beard."

Captain Banana Beard always kept bananas in his beard. That was how he got his name.

But Mr. Pickles didn't argue. "Aye, Captain," he said. *Aye* was monkey-pirate talk for *yes*.

"Careful, lad," the captain warned. "Or I'll feed you to the octo-shark." He turned and walked away.

"Aye-aye, Captain," Mr. Pickles replied.

"Don't worry," Fossey told Mr. Pickles. "There's no such thing as an octo-shark."

"Yo-ho-hold on a minute!" Captain Banana Beard stopped in his tracks. "No such thing as an octo-shark?!" he said.

"A beast that is half octopus and half shark?" Fossey asked. "Really?"

"Begging the captain's pardon," said Fez. "But we thought the octo-shark was something you made up to scare . . . ," he looked at Mr. Pickles, ". . . the crew."

"You don't believe in it, eh?" Captain Banana Beard grinned. "Well then, that be our next adventure. We'll hunt the octo-shark!"

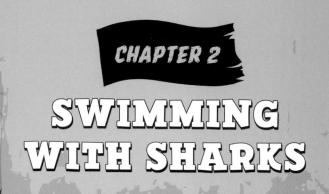

CHAPTER 2

SWIMMING WITH SHARKS

That night, everyone met in the captain's quarters. Musty maps covered his desk.

"'Twas long ago when I first laid eyes on the octo-shark," the captain said. "I was sailing alone when it attacked. It grabbed at me with its slimy arms. But I fought back."

"What happened then, Captain?" Mr. Pickles asked.

"I got away," the captain replied. "But not before it bit off one of me arms and both me legs."

"Uh . . . begging the captain's pardon," said Fez. "But you still have both arms and both legs."

Captain Banana Beard glanced down at himself and then back to Fez. "Well, I got better. Didn't I?"

Fez sighed. "Aye, Captain."

"So where can we find this octo-shark?" Fossey asked.

"Where else but . . . ," the captain pointed to a map, ". . . Shark Island!"

The next morning, the *Merry Monkey* arrived at Shark Island. Shark fins moved through the water.

Captain Banana Beard called from side of the ship, "Excuse me!"

"What was that, friend?" asked a passing shark.

"It's so hard to hear you from way down here," said another.

Mr. Pickles said, "Uh . . . Captain."

The captain stood upright. "Not now, Mr. Pickles," he said.

As Banana Beard stood, a shark jumped out of the water and snapped at him. The captain was nearly shark food!

But he didn't notice. He leaned back over the rail. "I said 'Excuse me!'" he repeated louder.

Fez marched toward
Captain Banana Beard.
"Captain, you have to
be careful."

Just then, Fez tripped
and bumped into the
captain. They
tumbled over the
railing.
SPLASH!

The captain and Fez floated in the water. Sharks surrounded them.

"Ah, that's better," said a grinning shark. "I'll hear you much better now."

Fez's teeth chattered with fear.

"We're looking for the dreaded octo-shark," the captain said. "Can you help us?"

The sharks glanced at each other. "What's an octo-shark?" one of them asked.

"P-p-part octopus, part sh-sh-shark," Fez stuttered with fright.

The sharks glanced at each other again. Then they roared with laughter.

"Did you hear that?" one of the sharks asked. "They're looking for an octo-shark!"

The sharks still laughed as Fossey and Mr. Pickles pulled Fez and Captain Banana Beard out of the water.

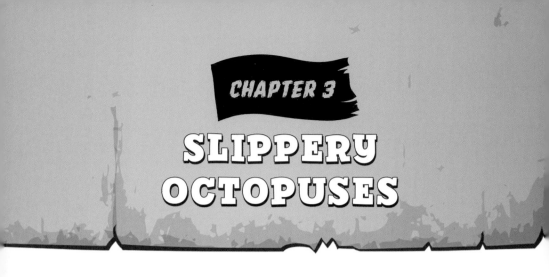

CHAPTER 3

SLIPPERY OCTOPUSES

"Sharks can't be trusted," the captain said.

He toweled off his bushy beard. He pretended not to notice as a few bananas fell out.

"What now, Captain?" asked Fossey.

"We search for the other half of the octo-shark," Banana Beard said. "Set sail for Octopus Garden!"

"Aye-aye, Captain!" said Fossey, Fez, and Mr. Pickles.

By the end of the day, the ship reached another tiny island. Octopus Garden wasn't a normal garden. It was actually the seafloor beside the small island.

"The octopuses live underwater," Mr. Pickles said. "How will we talk to them?"

"Simple," Captain Banana Beard replied. "We'll catch them."

He turned to Fossey. "Ready the coconut shells!"

"Aye-aye, Captain," Fossey said. She disappeared below deck.

"To catch an octopus, you first lower a hollow shell to the ocean floor," the captain explained. "The octopus goes inside. It thinks it be a nice new home. Then you

pull the shell out of the water!"

Fossey returned with several coconut halves tied together.

"Lower the coconuts," the captain ordered.

Fossey, Fez, and Mr. Pickles tossed them overboard.

Plop! Ploop! Plop!

After waiting a bit, the captain gave the order. "Haul them up!"

Everyone pulled the rope. The coconuts soon appeared. The pirates placed them carefully onto the deck.

An octopus crawled out of one of the hollow coconuts. "Oh my," it said, looking around. "Bad neighborhood."

Captain Banana Beard stepped forward. "I wonder if you can help us find the—"

"Excuse me. Pardon me," said the octopus.

The octopus slithered past the monkeys. It pulled itself over the rail and back into the water. **Plop!**

More octopuses crawled from coconuts. "Excuse me. Pardon me. Comin' through," they all said. Each one slinked to the ship's rail and flung themselves over.

Plop-plop! Ploop! Plop!

Captain Banana Beard sighed. "There be no trusting octopuses either," he said.

CHAPTER 4

SEEING IS BELIEVING

"Uh, Captain?" said Mr. Pickles. "It's OK if you made up the octo-shark. It was a good story."

The captain stomped over to Mr. Pickles. "Have you ever heard someone say, 'seeing is believing'?"

Mr. Pickles nodded. "Yes, sir."

"Well, lad." The captain smiled. "Some things have to be believed to be seen."

Mr. Pickles nodded again. "Aye, Captain."

"Now, Fez," said the captain. "I need a volunteer from the crew to act as bait."

"Aye-aye, Captain," Fez said. He turned to Fossey. "We need a volunteer from the crew."

Fossey turned to Mr. Pickles. "Are there any volunteers?"

Mr. Pickles glanced around. All eyes were on him. He gulped and raised his hand. "I volunteer?"

Captain Banana Beard patted him on the back. "That's a good lad!"

Fossey quickly built a giant fishing pole. Mr. Pickles fumbled with a long rope, trying to tie it around his waist.

"All right, bring him about," the captain ordered.

Fossey and Fez grabbed the end of the long pole. They swung it out over the ship.

But Mr. Pickles hadn't finished tying his knot. The rope tangled around the captain's legs instead.

Banana Beard was swept over the side of the ship!

"OK, OK!" the captain shouted. He dangled above the water. "I admit it. I made the whole thing up. There is no octo-shark!"

CREEEEEAK!

Suddenly the ship creaked and groaned. Eight giant octopus arms slithered onto the deck. A giant shark's head appeared after them.

"I believe in the octo-shark, Captain," Mr. Pickles said. "Because there it is!"

CHAPTER 5

ATTACK OF THE OCTO-SHARK

"We're under attack!" Fez shouted.

"What's going on?" asked the captain. "Get me down from here! Now!"

Two long octo-shark arms pointed at Fez and Fossey. The creature bared his sharp teeth.

"What have we here?" asked the octo-shark. "Two tasty treats?"

Then the beast spotted Captain Banana Beard dangling over his head. "*Three* tasty treats!" he said with a lick.

Banana Beard tried to wiggle free. "You'll not defeat me, beastie!"

As the captain struggled, bananas fell from his beard. They plopped into the octo-shark's mouth.

"What were those?" asked the octo-shark. "They were delicious."

"I don't know what you're talking about." The captain crossed his arms. "Nothing fell out of me beard. That's for sure."

"Those were bananas," Mr. Pickles replied. He held a banana barrel over his head. "And there's more where that came from!"

Mr. Pickles hurled the barrel into the octo-shark's mouth. The beast bit down, and the barrel exploded.

Bananas went everywhere! Luckily, most of them slid down the octo-shark's throat.

Nom-nom-nom!

After it had finished its snack, the octo-shark grabbed Captain Banana Beard. It placed him back onto the ship.

"That was quite tasty. Thank you," the octo-shark said. It wiped its mouth with one of its slimy arms. "I would eat you all, but I'm a bit full from all those bananas."

With that, the octo-shark turned and swam away.

"Well done, Mr. Pickles," said the captain. "But look at this mess." He pointed to the banana-covered deck.

The captain turned to Fez. "Have the crew swab the deck, Fez."

Fez turned to Fossey. "Have the crew swab the deck, Fossey."

Fossey turned to Mr. Pickles. "Swab the deck, Mr. Pickles."

Mr. Pickles gave a salute. "Aye-aye!"

As Fez followed Captain Banana Beard, Fossey stayed behind.

"Remember what the captain said," Fossey said to Mr. Pickles. "Some things have to be believed to be seen." She gave him a wink. "Well, I believe you'll be a great pirate someday."

ABOUT THE AUTHOR

Michael Anthony Steele has been in the entertainment industry for more than twenty years. He has worked in several capacities of film and television production from props and special effects all the way up to writing and directing. For many years, Mr. Steele has written exclusively for family entertainment. For television and video, he wrote for shows including *WISHBONE*, *Barney & Friends*, and *Boz, The Green Bear Next Door*. He has authored more than one hundred books for various characters and brands including *Batman*, *Green Lantern*, *LEGO City*, *Spider-Man*, *The Hardy Boys*, *Garfield*, and *Night at the Museum*.

ABOUT THE ILLUSTRATOR

Pauline Reeves lives by the sea in southwest England, with her husband, two children, and dog Jenson. She has loved drawing and creating since she was a child. Following her passion, Ms. Reeves graduated from Plymouth College of Art with a degree in illustration, and she specializes in children's literature. She takes inspiration from the funny and endearing things animals and people do every day. Ms. Reeves works both digitally and with traditional materials to create quirky illustrations with humor and charm.

GLOSSARY

bait (BAYT)—something, such as food, used to attract an animal so you can catch it

deck (DEK)—floor of a boat or ship

mast (MAST)—tall pole that stands on the floor of a boat or ship and supports its sails

pardon (PAR-duhn)—forgiveness

quarters (KWOR-ters)—lodgings or room where people live

slithered (SLITH-urd)—slipped and slid along like a snake

SHARE WITH YOUR MATEYS

1. Mr. Pickles volunteers to be the bait to catch the octo-shark. How do you think he felt?

2. Do you think that Captain Banana Beard is a good leader? Why or why not?

FOR YOUR PIRATE LOG

1. The octo-shark is a combination of an octopus and a shark. What are some other cool animal combinations you can make to create all new beasts? Make a list.

2. At the end of the story, Fossey tells Mr. Pickles that she thinks he will "be a great pirate someday." Write a short thank-you letter to Fossey from Mr. Pickles. What do you think he might say?

3. Pretend you are a monkey pirate, and there is treasure buried in your house! Draw a map and make sure to label all the places you can in order to make your map as detailed as possible. Mark the treasure with a banana!

THE SHIP DOESN'T STOP HERE!

Discover more at www.capstonekids.com

- ◡ VIDEOS & CONTESTS
- ◡ GAMES & PUZZLES
- ◡ FRIENDS & FAVORITES
- ◡ AUTHORS & ILLUSTRATORS